Tom and Ricky
and the
Silver Skateboard
Mystery

Bob Wright

High Noon Books
Novato, California

Cover Design: Nancy Peach
Interior Illustrations: Herb Heidinger

Glossary: contest, raft, store, either, tricks, winner, stranger, field

International Standard Book Number: 0-87879-393-3

10 09 08 07 06 05 04 03
15 14 13 12 11 10 9   8   7

Contents

CHAPTER 1

The Skateboard Contest

Tom was in a hurry. He had just read about it.
He wanted to let Ricky know.

"Ricky! Ricky!" Tom called.

"What is it?" Ricky called back.

"Come on out here," Tom called back.

Ricky came out of his house. "What's up?"
he asked.

"Have you heard about it?" Tom asked.

"Heard about what?" Ricky answered.

"The skateboard contest," Tom said.

"The skateboard contest? No. What's it all about?" Ricky asked.

"Mrs. Rose was on TV this morning. She was talking about it," Tom said.

"You mean Mrs. Rose from Rose's Gift Store?" Ricky asked.

"That's the one. They are going to have it next Saturday. They are going to give away lots of things," Tom said.

"Wait. Slow down. What's this all about?" Ricky asked.

"Mrs. Rose has a silver skateboard," Tom said.

"Silver skateboard? Are you kidding?" Ricky asked.

"No. She really does. She showed it on TV this morning. It is going to be at her store for a week," Tom said.

"I bet it cost a lot of money," Ricky said.

"It sure did. You should see it," Tom said.

"How can we see it?" Ricky said.

"It is going to be at her store starting today," Tom said.

"Tell me more about the contest," Ricky said.

"They are going to close off Link Street next Saturday. You have to let Mrs. Rose know if you want to be in the contest," Tom said.

"That sounds like fun. Want to be in it?" Ricky asked.

"I sure do. It sounds like fun. How about you?" Tom asked.

"You bet I do," Ricky answered.

"I have an idea. Let's skateboard over to Mrs. Rose's store. I haven't been on my skateboard for a long time," Tom said.

"That's a good idea. We can take a look at the silver skateboard," Ricky said.

"Then we can skateboard over to the creek. We need to do some work on the raft," Tom said.

"That's right. I forgot about the raft. Do you think it's still there?" Ricky asked.

"I sure hope so. We did a lot of work on that raft. It better be there," Tom said.

"Wait. I'll get my skateboard. Then we'll get yours. Then we can go over to Mrs. Rose's store," Ricky said.

Ricky went in the house. He called out to his mother. "Mom, I'm going to take my skateboard. I'm going with Tom. We're going over to Mrs. Rose's store."

"OK. Don't be gone too long," she called back.

Ricky got out his skateboard. "Come on, Tom. We'll go to your house. Then we'll go see that silver skateboard," Ricky said.

The two of them started for Tom's house. Tom was on his dirt bike. Ricky was on his skateboard.

CHAPTER 2

The Silver Skateboard

Tom jumped off his bike. He ran into his house and got his own skateboard. He and Ricky started down Front Street to Mrs. Rose's store.

"I haven't been on my skateboard for a long time," Tom said.

"I haven't been on mine either. I think I'll try a few tricks," Ricky said.

Ricky tried riding with one foot. Then he tried the other. He tried turning.

"That looks good, Ricky," Tom called out.

"You try some tricks," Ricky called back.

"I will. I will. I need to get used to it again,"
Tom called out.

Ricky tried riding with one foot.
Then he tried the other.

There were a lot of people shopping on Front Street. There were a lot of kids on skateboards.

"Look at all the kids on skateboards. Everyone heard about the contest," Ricky said.

There was a big sign on Rose's Gift Store. It said, "SKATEBOARD CONTEST NEXT SATURDAY."

"Look at that sign," Tom said.

"Now I know why there are so many kids on skateboards," Ricky said.

"Look at all the police around Rose's Gift Store," Tom said.

"I bet the silver skateboard is there," Ricky said.

"Look! There's Sergeant Collins," Tom said.

They both skateboarded over to their friend Sergeant Collins.

"I'll bet you're both here to sign up for the skateboard contest," the Sergeant said.

"We sure are," Tom said.

"Is the silver skateboard here yet?" Ricky asked.

"It just got here. Look at all the people. We are going to have to be here all week. That skateboard cost a lot of money. We don't want anyone to take it," the Sergeant said.

"We're going to sign up for the contest," Tom said.

"We'll see you later," Ricky said.

"OK. Take care," their friend said.

"Look at that long line. Everyone in town is waiting to sign up," Tom said.

"Do you want to come back later? There won't be as many people then," Ricky said.

"That's a good idea. We can go to the creek. Then we'll come back," Tom said.

Tom and Ricky started off for the creek.

CHAPTER 3

The Raft

Tom and Ricky started down Front Street. That was the fast way to the creek. They carried their skateboards down to the creek.

"Look. There it is. It's still safe," Tom said.

"Let's see if it is still all together," Ricky said.

They walked over to the creek. There were a lot of leaves on the raft. But it was still on the water.

"It looks OK to me," Tom said.

"I think I'll stand on it to make sure," Ricky said.

Ricky stepped on to the raft. It went down a little into the water. Then he stepped off.

"Tom, that raft won't even hold me. We still need to make it bigger. Get some more small logs. I'll get that rope we hid," Ricky said.

Tom went to look for some small logs. Ricky got the rope he hid in a tree near the creek.

Then Tom came back with some small logs. They tied them together.

"We need to get into the water. Take off your shoes and socks. Roll up your pants. The water isn't deep here," Ricky said.

"OK," Tom said.

They both stepped into the water.

"Be careful. Even though the water isn't deep, these rocks are easy to fall on," Ricky said.

Ricky stepped on to the raft.
It went down a little into the water.

They took the small logs Tom had gotten. They tied them on to the raft.

Tom stood back. "That looks pretty good to me," he said.

"Yes, it does. But will it hold us?" Ricky said.

"Let's find out," Tom said.

This time Tom stood on it. The raft didn't sink. It stayed on top of the water.

"Now you get on with me," Tom said.

Ricky stepped on to the raft.

"It's going down just a little," Ricky said.

Water came up over on to the raft. Ricky stepped off back into the low water.

"Well, we know one thing," Ricky said.

"What's that?" Tom asked.

"It will hold only one of us. Be careful," Ricky said.

"This water isn't deep. Let me see if I can take it out a little way," Tom said.

Ricky gave the raft a little push. The raft stayed on the water. Then Tom made it come back to where Ricky was.

"Let's pull it out of the water," Ricky said.

"That's right. We have to get back and sign up for the contest," Tom said.

They pulled the raft out of the creek. They left it next to a tall tree.

"Come on. Let's sit and let our feet dry off," Ricky said.

They walked over to a big log and sat down.

"What are they going to give the winner of the skateboard contest?" Ricky asked.

"For one thing, the winner gets to ride on the silver skateboard," Tom said.

"Anything else?" Ricky asked.

"Mrs. Rose is going to give away a lot of things. The winner will get the most," Tom said.

"It sounds like a lot of fun. But it will be hard to win," Ricky said.

"It will be. There are a lot of good skateboarders in town," Tom said.

"My feet are dry. How about yours?" Ricky asked.

"They're dry. Let's get our shoes and socks on," Tom said.

"That line at Mrs. Rose's store should be short by now. We won't have such a long wait," Ricky said.

"Right. Let's get going," Tom said.

They picked up their skateboards and started back.

CHAPTER 4

Two Strangers

Tom and Ricky started back. They wanted to get signed up for the skateboard contest. They started walking away from the creek.

"Tom, let's take the short cut," Ricky said.

That's a good idea. We won't be able to use our skateboards. But it will be faster," Ricky said.

"We can cut across the field. That way we'll end up almost right at Mrs. Rose's store," Tom said.

"Boy, this grass is high," Tom said.

"It sure is. Maybe we should have gone the other way," Ricky said.

"Look. I see some men coming this way," Tom said.

"Maybe they're taking the short cut, too," Ricky said.

The men walked over to Tom and Ricky. One of them said, "Where does this field end up?"

"Over by the creek," Tom said.

"Is there anything near the creek?" the man asked.

"No. On the other side of the creek there are woods," Ricky said.

"Have you boys been fishing?" the man asked.

"Not today," Ricky answered.

"On the other side of the creek there are woods," Ricky said.

"No. Sometimes we do fish there. Today we were working on our raft," Tom said.

"When I was a kid, I made a raft," the man said.

"We made a good one. Next time we're here we can use it," Ricky said.

"Are you going to be in the skateboard contest next Saturday?" the man asked.

"We sure are. We both want to win something," Tom said.

"I bet you will. But there are going to be a lot of people trying to win," the man said.

"Do you live around here?" Tom asked.

The two men looked at each other. "No. We're here for the contest," one of them said.

"Do you work for Mrs. Rose?" Ricky asked.

"No. We're here to see that the silver skateboard will be safe," the man said.

"We've got to go now. We still need to sign up for the contest," Tom said.

"We're going to walk over to the creek. We'll see you the day of the contest," the man said. Then the two men started to walk over to the creek.

"Come on, Tom. Let's get going," Ricky said.

"Look. There's the back of Mrs. Rose's store. This was much faster," Tom said.

They walked around the store to Front Street. There were lots of kids on skateboards.

"Look at that," Ricky said.

"You mean all those people riding their skateboards?" Tom asked.

"Yes, that. But a lot of them are painted silver," Ricky said.

"That's right. What's that all about?" Tom said.

"I don't know. Let's find out when we sign up," Ricky said.

CHAPTER 5

The Sign Up

Tom and Ricky went over to Mrs. Rose's Gift Store. The line wasn't long any more. They saw their friend Sergeant Collins. He was near the store.

"Have you signed up yet?" Sergeant Collins asked Tom and Ricky.

"Not yet. We're going to do it right now," Ricky said.

"There was a long line this morning. There were lots of people here," the Sergeant said.

"Look at all the skateboards. Why are they silver?" Tom asked.

"Someone thought it would be a good idea. Everyone is buying silver paint. This is really turning into a big thing," the Sergeant said.

"What do you think, Ricky? Should we paint ours?" Tom asked.

"No. I want to leave mine just the way it is," Ricky said.

"Me, too," Tom said.

"Who are all those men at Mrs. Rose's store?" Ricky asked.

"Mrs. Rose got five men to help her. She doesn't want anything to happen to that silver skateboard," the Sergeant said.

"Come on, Ricky. Let's get over there," Tom said.

Tom and Ricky got in the line in front of Mrs. Rose's store. They didn't have to wait long. Mrs. Rose was busy. She was doing the sign ups.

"Well, hello, Tom and Ricky," she said.

"Hi, Mrs. Rose. I bet you've had a busy day," Ricky said.

"I sure have. But I'm glad you are both going to be in the contest next Saturday. Have you seen the silver skateboard yet?" she asked.

"No. Where is it?" Ricky asked.

"It's right over there. You can take a good look at it after you sign up. I'm glad I have those five big men to help me," she said.

Tom and Ricky looked over. They could see part of the silver skateboard. The five men were standing around it.

"Boy, those men sure are big. Look at them," Tom said.

"They have to make sure no one takes the skateboard," Ricky said.

"Here. Write your name, your age, and your address on these papers. Then drop them in this box. Good luck," she said.

"Thanks, Mrs. Rose," Ricky said.

Tom and Ricky took the papers. They filled them out. Then they dropped them in the box.

"Come on, Ricky. Now let's see that silver skateboard," Tom said.

Tom and Ricky walked over to look at the silver skateboard. It shone in the sunlight. The five big men stood close to it.

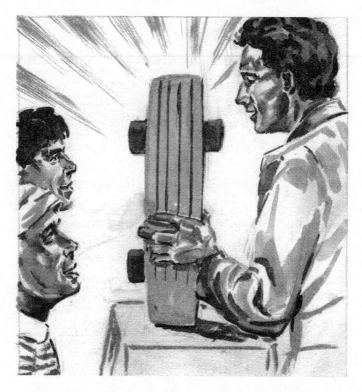

"It cost a lot of money," the man said.

One of them looked at Ricky. "Would you like to have that?" he asked.

"I sure would," Ricky said.

"It cost a lot of money," the man said.

"I can see that," Ricky answered.

"Are you going to paint your skateboard silver?" the man asked.

"No. I don't think so," Ricky said.

"OK, boys. You'll have to move on. Other people want to take a look now," the man said.

Tom and Ricky started to go.

"Those men look like football players. Boy, they are big," Ricky said.

"I don't think anyone will try to take that skateboard," Tom said.

CHAPTER 6

Getting Ready

Tom and Ricky started to go back to Ricky's house.

"Come on, Tom. Let's go back to Page Street. There aren't as many cars and people there," Ricky said.

"That's a good idea. We can work on our skateboarding there," Tom said.

"Look. There are those two men we saw in back of Mrs. Rose's store," Ricky said.

"They are the same ones," Tom said.

The two men saw Tom and Ricky. They walked over to them.

"You boys were right," one of the men said.

"Right about what?" Ricky asked.

"About that raft. It is a good one," the man said.

"Did you get on it?" Tom asked.

"No, no, no. We just looked at it," the man said very fast.

Then the other man said," That is a fast way to get to the creek. Do many people know about that short cut?"

"A lot of the kids do. But most people take the long way. They go up Front Street to get to the creek," Ricky said.

"They don't like to walk through all that grass," Tom said.

"I can see why. You can really get dirty," the man said.

"I bet you're going back to help Mrs. Rose," Tom said.

"Help Mrs. Rose? Oh, yes. That's right. We have to get back to the store. They need us there," the man said.

"We'll see you around," Tom said.

"You know, something is funny," Ricky said.

"What do you mean?" Tom asked.

"Those two men. They don't look like the other men at Mrs. Rose's store," Ricky said.

"That's right. The men at the store are really big," Tom said.

"And another thing. Sergeant Collins said Mrs. Rose had five men to help her. That's how many men there were at the store. All five of them were there," Ricky said.

"That's right. I don't get it. What's going on?" Tom said.

"Something strange is going on. Maybe we should find Sergeant Collins and tell him," Ricky said.

"But we don't have anything to go on. We saw two men. They were in the big field. They walked over to the creek. Then we saw them again," Tom said.

"But they said they worked for Mrs. Rose. And Sergeant Collins told us that Mrs. Rose only had five men working for her. And we saw those men at her store," Ricky said.

"Let's keep our eyes on those two men. We'll see them again around town this week," Tom said.

"That's a good idea. Let's see if they do work for Mrs. Rose," Ricky said.

Tom and Ricky kept going to Page Street where Ricky lived. It wasn't far. They wanted to get ready for the big skateboard contest.

CHAPTER 7

The Big Contest

The day of the skateboard contest came. Tom met Ricky on Page Street.

"Come on, Ricky. Get your skateboard. Let's get going," Tom called out.

"OK, OK. I'm all ready," Ricky called back.

The two boys started to go up Page Street.

"You should see all the people. There are no cars on Front Street," Tom said.

"I bet there are a lot of silver skateboards," Ricky said.

"There sure are. I think that almost half of them are silver," Tom said.

"Where will the contest begin?" Ricky asked.

"They want everyone to go to the end of Link Street. They will go by ages," Tom said.

"What do you mean?" Ricky asked.

"The first race will be the six-year-old kids. Then the next will be the seven-year-olds. We'll have to wait for the fourteen-year-olds, but it won't take long," Tom said.

"Which way will they go?" Ricky asked.

"They will start on Link Street. Then they will turn on to Front Street. That will be right in front of Mrs. Rose's store," Tom said.

"Where will it end?" Ricky asked.

"Here on Page Street," Tom said.

Up on Front Street they saw Sergeant Collins. He called out to them.

"Look. There's Sergeant Collins. I think he is calling to us," Ricky said.

They ran over to him.

"You sure look busy," Tom said.

"I am. There are a lot of police out today," the Sergeant said.

"There sure are. They are all over the place," Ricky said.

"Have you boys seen anything strange?" the Sergeant asked.

"What do you mean?" Ricky asked.

"We got a tip that someone is going to try to take the silver skateboard," he answered.

"What about those two men, Ricky?" Tom asked.

"That's right. We haven't seen them all week long. I forgot about them," Ricky said.

"What's that all about?" the Sergeant asked.

Ricky told Sergeant Collins about seeing the men. He told him what the two strange men said about working for Mrs. Rose.

"I don't like any of this. Keep your eyes out for those two men. If you see them, let me know," the Sergeant said.

"We sure will. Come on, Tom. We have to get up to Link Street," Ricky said.

Tom and Ricky picked up their tags. The tags meant they were signed up for the contest. Soon it was time for the fourteen-year-olds to race.

All the boys lined up. When they heard "GO!" they all started down Link Street. Tom and Ricky were near the front. "Keep moving, Tom," Ricky called out.

They got to the end of Link Street. When they were turning on to Front Street Tom called to Ricky. "Look, Ricky. The two strange men. They are running down Front Street. They have something."

"It looks like a skateboard. It's the silver skateboard," Ricky called back.

There were a lot of people. The police were running after the men.

"The men are going in back of Mrs. Rose's," Tom said.

Tom saw Sergeant Collins. "They're going to the big field. They're going to the big field," Tom yelled.

Sergeant Collins called the five big men and some other police. They all ran with Tom and Ricky into the big field.

"How do you know they are going this way?" Sergeant Collins called to Ricky.

"This is where we saw them. They wanted to know how many people knew this short cut," Ricky yelled back.

They saw the two men with the silver skateboard. They weren't far ahead. The skateboard was shining in the sun.

"That skateboard is very heavy. It will slow them down," the Sergeant yelled.

"Ricky! Ricky! They're running over to our raft," Tom yelled.

The two men ran down to the creek.

One of them yelled, "Get on that raft. We'll push it out down the creek. They'll never get us."

Sergeant Collins was running. He looked down to the creek. He saw the two men pushing the raft out into the water.

The raft got out on the water. Then it started to go down into the water.

"These two men are too heavy. That silver skateboard is too heavy. Look, the raft is sinking," Ricky said.

"That silver skateboard is too heavy. Look, the raft is sinking," Ricky said.

The two men started to yell. "Help us. We can't swim. Help! Help!"

By that time the police, the five men from the store, and Tom and Ricky were down at the creek.

The two men were sitting in the water.

"It's only three feet deep," Ricky said.

The two men in the water were all muddy.

One of them said, "I told you not to use this raft!"

"You two come with me," Sergeant Collins said.

The two men got out of the water.

"Where's the silver skateboard?" Tom asked.

"Go get it yourself. It's in the water," one of the men said.

"You bet I will," Tom said. He jumped in the water and got the silver skateboard.

Ricky jumped in, too.

"Well. You boys didn't win the race. But you get to do something no one else will do," Sergeant Collins said.

"What's that?" Tom asked.

"You get to carry the silver skateboard back to Mrs. Rose's store," Sergeant Collins answered.

"What a day!" Ricky yelled.